101 Corona Virus Jokes
Or
Laughing Your Way
Through Troubled Times

Dear Readers,

There is no doubt that the outbreak of COVID-19, also known as the Corona Virus is a very serious issue. However, I was raised to believe that if you can't laugh even at the toughest of times, then you end up crying your eyes at.

I hope all of my readers will know that this joke book is not about minimizing the crisis, it's about sharing the human stress-reliever of laughter at an incredibly difficult time.

Let's all hope that laughter is indeed the best medicine.

Sincerely,

Dr. H

1.

A man goes into the doctor's office to be tested for the Corona Virus. The doctor returns with the test results and says:

"I'm sorry to inform you that you have tested possible for the virus. We're going to need to quarantine you at home for 14 days, restricted to one room and begin you on a diet of bologna and cheese."

"Why?" the man asked. "Will those foods specifically help me fight the virus?"

"Oh, no." the doctor replied. "They're just the only foods that will fit under the door."

2.

The police got called out to a cabin where they'd received a call saying that a man with Corona Virus was ignoring his quarantine and running through the woods in his front yard. When they arrived they saw the man not just wandering the front yard but also completely naked. Slightly afraid to approach him, the police used the car's megaphone.

"Sir, you must return inside to resume your quarantine!" the officer's voice boomed.

"I can't go back in yet!" The man shouted back, "I'm trying to get as many ticks on me as possible."

Confused the officer asked through the megaphone "Sir, why would you be trying to get covered in ticks?"

"Because I prefer my Corona with Lyme!"

3.

It's a shame all of these potential Corona Virus patients are stuck at the airport trying to get home from Europe. It's going to cause a terminal illness.

4.

My wife came down with Corona Virus and now the dishwasher isn't working. But she'll be back on her feet in a week or so.

5.

A doctor walked into a hospital room where a patient was lying on a bed connected to a ventilator.

"Miss Johnson, I'm sorry to inform you that your Corona Virus has progressed and it's possible you may only have a week to live depending on treatment." The doctor said, gravely.

"What? There must be something I can do about it?" the woman sobbed.

"Well, you could marry an accountant." The doctor replied.

"How will that help me live longer than a week?" the woman asked, confused.

"It won't." The doctor answered, "But it'll make it feel like forever."

6.

A man diagnosed with the Corona Virus was desperate for a cure and scouring the internet for any kind of experimental remedy. Finally, he picked one and, following the instructions, went to the very top of a steep grassy incline and covered himself with butter. He went downhill pretty fast after that.

7.

A man called the doctor to check on how his elderly mother, who had been diagnosed with the Corona Virus, was doing in the hospital. As he listened to the doctor's response he nodded somberly and then hung the phone up.

"Is it bad?" his wife asked, nervously.

"We have to prepare the guest room; your mother might be coming to live with us starting today." the man answered.

"How is that possible?" the wife replied. "She's at the hospital on a ventilator."

"I don't know." The husband responded, "But the Dr. said we had to prepare for the worst."

8.

They say smoking makes the Corona Virus much worse, but it can cure salmon.

9.

A doctor walks into the waiting room and says to a woman "I'm sorry, but your husband either has Corona Virus or Alzheimer's."

"Well how do I know which one it is?" she asks.

"Take him to the park after this, then head home. If he finds his way back, it's Corona Virus."

10.

During the Corona Virus outbreak, please don't cough or sneeze without a tissue, you'd be taking matters into your own hands.

11.

An English teacher was comparing two different things for his students when he sneezed and suddenly worried that he might have the Corona Virus, but it turns out he just had analogy.

12.

My friend irritated me when he tried to cheer me up about the Corona Virus by saying "it could be worse, you could be stuck in a hole in the ground filled with water", but I know he means well.

13.

The invisible man wasn't at all afraid during the Corona Virus outbreak, he just couldn't see himself getting it.

14.

The muffler didn't feel well and was convinced he had the Corona Virus, but it turned out he was just exhausted.

15.

Someone on the internet said that you can cure the Corona Virus by eating nothing but almonds, but frankly that's just nuts.

16.

Given the rules of social distancing during the Corona Virus outbreak a half-cocked entrepreneur decided to open a restaurant on the moon. It didn't work out, though, because while the food was actually pretty good, it had no atmosphere.

17.

A natural healer told me that I could avoid the Corona Virus if I made tea out of the leaves of a dogwood tree. I googled how to know if a tree was a dogwood, turns out you can tell by the bark.

18.

There is a rumor going around that you can cure the Corona Virus by covering yourself in mayonnaise, but I'm not going to spread it.

19.

I asked my doctor what Covid-19 stood for and he told me it was because it got tired of sitting.

20.

I tried to come up with a joke about why retired people are at higher risk of Corona Virus, but none of them work.

21.

Do you know that the Corona Virus weighs less than one thousandth of a gram? I mean, 0mg.

22.

A doctor walked into a Corona Virus patient's room and said, "I'm sorry but you only have 10 more to live." When the patient asked, "weeks or days?" the doctor responded "9,8,7..."

23.

A doctor walked into the room and said, "bad news, turns out you have both Corona Virus and Alzheimer's." to which the patient responded, "Well at least I don't have that Corona Virus."

24.

There was a doctor who got very frustrated how long it took his slow nurse to do a Corona Virus swab...she really tested his patients.

25.

Two teenagers had been dating for about a week when the young man came down with flulike symptoms. The young woman got very nervous, so she asked him to go be tested for the Corona Virus. He came back and said, "I've got good news and bad news, which do you want first?"

"The good news." She replied.

"My test came back negative." He answered.

She was so happy that she ran and kissed him right on the mouth and said, "I'm so glad, so what's the bad news?"

"I lied." he answered.

26.

The archeology student was thrilled when she learned that she didn't have Corona Virus and would be able to graduate, but then she realized that her future was still in ruins.

27.

There was a hippie that was so nervous he decided to take his Corona Virus test while high on magic mushrooms, turns out he passed with flying colors.

<u>28.</u>

When the nurse handed me the swab to take the Corona Virus test, I put it in my mouth and swallowed it. She asked me why I did that and I explained that now I was guaranteed to eventually pass the test.

29.

A woman came back to the doctor for a follow up after she'd recovered from the Corona Virus.

"How are you feeling today?" the doctor asked.

"Ok physically," she replied, "but still a little upset about the divorce."

"I'm so sorry to hear you got a divorce." The doctor replied.

"Well you told me I had to cut out anything alcoholic if I wanted to recover."

30.

When re-entering the country from the Corona Virus scare an American tourist had to fill out forms and be examined. When he was done, the nurse examining him made a few notes on a clipboard and asked, "And who should we contact in case of an emergency?" He replied, "A very good doctor, please."

31.

The nurse tried explaining to the patient why they performed the Corona Virus test with a Q-tip, but it went in one ear and out the other.

32.

A doctor returned to the room and said to the patient "So your blood test came back and while you don't have the Corona Virus it looks like you're pregnant." She clasped her hands to her chest and said, "I'm pregnant?" to which the doctor replied, "No I just said it looks like you're pregnant."

33.

A woman's husband came down with the Corona Virus and was admitted to the hospital. A few hours later, she was sitting in the intensive care unit waiting room when a doctor came out and said, "I'm sorry ma'am, we did everything you asked."

"And?" the woman replied.

"He's still going to pull through."

<u>34.</u>

My elderly grandma has been asking me at weddings for years "So, do you think you'll be next?", so I've started asking her the same during the Corona Virus outbreak.

35.

A doctor calls a patient with Corona Virus and says "I'm sorry to tell you that I accidentally swapped your cough syrup prescription for a maximum strength laxative. I'll get it changed right away. I really apologize. Has the coughing been just awful?"

"Not at all." The patient replied. "Since about 30 minutes after I took that medicine, I've been too afraid to."

36.

Doctor: I'm sorry to tell you that you've tested positive for the Corona Virus.

Patient: I'd like to get a second opinion.

Doctor: Well you're not particularly attractive, either.

37.

The doctor handed his patient a very strong cough syrup to help with his Corona Virus and said, "I have to warn you that 9 out of 10 people who take this medicine suffer from diarrhea."

The patient replied "That 10th guy who enjoyed it must be a real weirdo."

38.

Nurse: Doctor, the invisible man is here demanding to be tested for the Corona Virus.

Doctor: Just tell him I can't see him right now.

39.

I went to buy toilet paper to get me through the Corona Virus shut down, but the store was all wiped out.

40.

Man, this Corona Virus outbreak really has people making Armageddon jokes like there's no tomorrow.

41.

Doctor: I'm afraid I only have bad news and very bad news.

Patient: Well, bad news first.

Doctor: Your Corona Virus has gotten worse and it's possible you have less than 24hours to live.

Patient: Oh my goodness, what on earth is the very bad news?

Doctor: I've been trying to reach you since yesterday.

42.

When I caught Corona Virus the doctor told me not to worry and that he'd have me on my feet in two or three weeks. He was right, I had to sell my car to pay the medical bill.

43.

Question: During the Corona Virus outbreak...does an apple a day really keep the doctor away?

Answer: Yes, but only if you have really good aim.

44.

The doctor tried to save the Corona Virus victim with an IV of fluids, but it was all in vein.

45.

There was a patient who was so sick with the Corona Virus that he lost feeling in his whole left side. But he's all right now.

46.

A woman calls the doctor to say that her daughter is trying to use some crazy remedy she found on the internet to deal with her Corona Virus symptoms.

"What is she doing?" the doctor asked.

"She just lays in bed all day and eats yeast and wax." The woman replied.

"That's excellent, it's bound to work." The doctor answered.

"Why on earth would you say that?" the mother begged.

"Because eventually she will rise and shine."

<u>47.</u>

A doctor saw a patient with the Corona Virus and told him the best way to treat it was every night to have two teaspoons of cough syrup and a warm bath. When the man came back the next week the doctor asked him how it was going, and he said "Terrible. I mean drinking the cough syrup isn't hard, but I can never finish the whole bath."

48.

A cup of espresso goes to the doctor and asks to be tested for the Corona Virus. When the doctor asks what symptoms have been occurring the cup of espresso says, "well I'm just a little coffee."

49.

I've decided to try a new herbal remedy for my Corona Virus because they always say that Thyme heals all wounds.

50.

A lizard walked into the doctor and said "Doc, I think I have the Corona Virus."

"Why do you think that? What are your symptoms?" the doctor asked.

"Well, for example," the lizard replied. "My penis isn't currently working."

"Oh, no, that's not the Corona Virus." The doctor answered. "That's just a reptile dysfunction."

51.

What does the Italian outbreak have in common with ravioli? They've both been pasta round.

52.

A Corona Virus walks into a bar. The bartender says "Hey, bud, we don't serve infectious diseases here." To which the virus replies "Well you're certainly not a very good host."

53.

Question: How can you tell the difference between the Corona Virus and a retrovirus?

Answer: the 70's haircut.

54.

I heard that new pop song about the Corona Virus. I thought it was pretty catchy.

55.

Why did the Shetland pony ask to take a Corona Virus test? He was a little horse.

56.

I've been coughing for the last two days. I'm afraid it could be the Corona Virus, or it could be pneumocystofibromisialgica, but it's hard to say.

57.

Doctor: Since you came down with the Corona Virus has your cough gotten any better?

Patient: I hope so, I've sure been practicing a lot.

58.

When you think about the spread of the Corona Virus, it's truly breathtaking.

59.

A man came down with the Corona Virus and his doctor walked him through the process of how to self-isolate. To make clear the severity of the issue the doctor said "Self-isolation is a necessity. Even at home it's important that you be six feet away from your wife at all times."

The man shook his head and said "This is going to be hard. I haven't been that close to her in fifteen years."

60.

An old pirate went to the doctor because he was terribly concerned that he was at exceptionally high risk for the Corona Virus. When the doctor asked him why he said, "Because Aye, Matey."

61.

A man walks into the doctor concerned that he's got the Corona Virus. "What are your symptoms?" the doctor asked.

"Just like I've read about, so many aches and pains. If I tough my leg it hurts, if I touch my head it hurts, if I touch my chest it hurts. Everything I touch hurts."

The doctor examined him briefly and said, "Turns out you have a broken finger."

62.

This whole Corona Virus thing had me feeling sad, lonely and depressed. But things are turning around...now I'm depressed, sad and lonely.

63.

Did you hear the one about the paranoid
man with the speech impediment during the
Corona Virus outbreak? He was worried
about the Apocalisp.

64.

Just recently doctors tested the first car to see if it had COVID-19, but it turns out it only had the Corolla Virus.

65.

A chicken decided to voluntarily self-isolate during the Corona Virus outbreak, but after a day or so she started to feel cooped up.

66.

I heard that the invisible man died from the Corona Virus because he couldn't get into the ICU.

67.

I've actually made a small fortune in the stock market during the Corona Virus outbreak...unfortunately I started with a large one.

68.

What does the FED interest rate have to do with the chance of our government handling the Corona Virus outbreak well? They're both near zero.

69.

I have this one Corona Virus joke that almost never gets a laugh when I tell it, but 2.4% of the time it kills.

70.

A man went the doctor for help with his Corona Virus symptoms and the doctor gave him a face mask and had him inhale helium. The man came back the next day and the doctor tried giving him curium. The next day the man called back to make a third appointment claiming he was still no better and the nurse said to the doctor "well you tried helium and curium I hope you don't have to barium."

71.

I was going to add a time travelling joke here about how the Corona Virus ends, but you didn't like it.

72.

Given the seriousness of the Corona Virus outbreak I have decided to quit drinking all together. Now I'm just drinking alone.

73.

During the panic of grocery shopping during the Corona Virus outbreak a security guard saw a guy trying to sneak out of the store with a whole leg of lamb.

"Hey, you!" the guard said. "What are you doing with that?"

The thief replied "Slow roasting it at 375 degrees with some potatoes and rosemary.

74.

I heard that doctors have been trying to heal Corona Virus by mixing the blood of healed patients in a blender and injecting it into the sick ones. So far, they're only getting mixed results.

75.

I wanted to be a good citizen to the medical industry during the Corona Virus outbreak, so I became a blood and plasma donor...but I didn't have the guts to become an organ donor.

76.

Given we are all self-isolating during the Corona Virus outbreak I'm thinking about taking up meditation. It'll be better than just sitting around doing nothing.

77.

I got so bored after twenty-four hours of self-isolation that I called it a day.

78.

I went to the pharmacy to get medicine for my Corona Virus symptoms and the cashier asked me if it wanted the cough syrup in a bag, but I told her to please leave it in the bottle.

79.

I'd tell you a joke about the temporary hospital they're building for the Corona Virus, but it's still under construction.

80.

I'm reading a book about the hypothesis that the Corona Virus can't live in a zero-gravity environment and it's impossible to put down.

81.

I think anyone with the Corona Virus should get a few extra comforters to keep warm through the chills...but I guess I shouldn't make blanket statements.

82.

My doctor told me to stay in bed until my Corona Virus cleared up, but I got so stir crazy I was up walking around the house instead of taking a nap, until my wife, who is a police officer, threated to charge me with resisting a rest.

83.

I was going to go to church to get some holy water to pray to stay safe from the Corona Virus, but they shut the church down as a precaution. The good news is I figured out how to make my own holy water, I just filled up a pot and boiled the hell out of it.

84.

Did you hear about the Corona Virus
outbreak at the circus? It was in tents.

85.

I had what felt was a terrible cold: sneezing, sinus congestion and my ears were so blocked I was having trouble hearing. I went to the doctor to make sure it wasn't the Corona Virus and the first thing he did was ask me to describe the symptoms. "That's easy," I said. "Homer is married to Marge and they have three kids: Bart, Maggie and Lisa."

<u>86.</u>

During the Corona Virus shut down I thought that it might be a good time to slim down and lose some weight. I thought I might try a really restricted diet, but then I realized I have too much on my plate right now.

87.

I went to the doctor to get tested for the Corona Virus and told the doctor that I was experiencing aches and pains in several places. He responded, "Well stop going to those places."

88.

I was trying to decide if there would be any advantages to going back home to Switzerland to ride out the Corona Virus outbreak. I mean I guess the flag is a big plus.

89.

I was wondering what COVID-19 was short for, but I realized it must just have tiny legs.

90.

I wanted to slim down while I'm practicing social distancing, so I decided that I'd eat no food and just drink Whiskey. I've lost 4 days already.

91.

I asked my doctor if it was safe to use a public pool during the Corona Virus outbreak. He told me it deep ends.

92.

I bought this special mask that was
supposed to prevent the Corona Virus, made
all out of Velcro, but it was a total rip-off.

93.

In light of the shortage during the Corona Virus outbreak I was gonna tell a joke about toilet paper, but it was tearable.

94.

To pinch pennies while riding out the Corona Virus outbreak I decided to collect all of the cans in my neighborhood and turn them in to the recycling center. I only made $13.50 after 8 hours of can crushing, it was soda pressing.

95.

My doctor told me that it might be hard to stay warm while I have the Corona Virus due to all of the chills and fever...so I pushed my bed into the corner, where it's 90 degrees.

96.

I was worried about having cash on hand during the Corona Virus outbreak so I stopped by the bank and asked the teller if she would check my balance…so she pushed me.

97.

I have a friend who is stuck on a cruise ship during this whole Corona Virus lockdown. They are totally quarantined to their rooms. They can't even play cards because the Captain is standing on the deck.

98.

I started thinking about how the Corona Virus was going to affect all of our lives, how it would make us think about the past, the present and the future...but I got all tense.

99.

As if the quarantine for the Corona Virus wasn't bad enough, then today I heard there was a kidnapping in our neighborhood. Eventually he woke up, though.

100.

I called my yoga teacher if she planned on breaking quarantine during the Corona Virus to have class but she said "Namaste here."

101.

My friend asked me if I was worried about getting my taxes done during the Corona Virus outbreak. I told him that I don't pay taxes...I'm an atheist so I count as a non-prophet.

TO MY READERS

I hope a few of these 101 jokes brightened your day and made you laugh. If none of them made you laugh, give the book to your Dad...he'll love 'em.

In today's digital world, online feedback and ratings play a vital, important role in getting the word out about new books and authors. If you would be willing to take just another moment out of your day to rate this book on Amazon or Goodreads or if you are so inspired to a review it, I would be extremely grateful. You have no idea how much these reviews can change a book's lifespan.

And in regards to COVID-19...hang in there. We'll get through this together.